Front endpapers by Cory Taylor aged 7
Back endpapers by Molly Heenan aged 7

Thank you to John King Infant School, Pinxton, Derbyshire
for creating the endpapers – K.P.

For Eve, who has given so many lovely parties – V.T.
For our daughter Zoë who is the same age as Winnie – K.P.

OXFORD
UNIVERSITY PRESS

Great Clarendon Street, Oxford OX2 6DP

Oxford University Press is a department of the University of Oxford.
It furthers the University's objective of excellence in research, scholarship,
and education by publishing worldwide in

Oxford New York

Auckland Cape Town Dar es Salaam Hong Kong Karachi
Kuala Lumpur Madrid Melbourne Mexico City Nairobi
New Delhi Shanghai Taipei Toronto

With offices in

Argentina Austria Brazil Chile Czech Republic France Greece
Guatemala Hungary Italy Japan Poland Portugal Singapore
South Korea Switzerland Thailand Turkey Ukraine Vietnam

Oxford is a registered trade mark of Oxford University Press
in the UK and in certain other countries

British Library Cataloguing in Publication Data

Data available

ISBN: 978-0-19-272737-4 (hardback)

Printed in Italy

www.korkypaul.com

Valerie Thomas and Korky Paul

Happy Birthday, Winnie!

OXFORD
UNIVERSITY PRESS

When Winnie the Witch turned over the page on her calendar, she saw a big red circle around Friday the thirteenth.

'That's my birthday!' she said.
'I'll have a party this year, Wilbur.'
'Purr,' said Wilbur. He loved parties.

'What kind of party?' Winnie wondered.
'I know, a garden party.'

On Monday Winnie wrote out the invitations
and sent them by Winni-e-mail.
She invited . . .

Aunty Alice,
Uncle Owen,
her three sisters Wanda, Wilma and Wendy,
all of her friends,
and Cousin Cuthbert.

On Tuesday she made herself a party dress,
and a matching bow for Wilbur.
'Purr,' said Wilbur. I look lovely, he thought.

On Wednesday Winnie made lots and lots of food.
Wilbur helped.

Thursday was the day to get the garden ready.
Winnie went outside. It looked rather scruffy.
Then Winnie had a very good idea.
She took out her wand, waved it, shouted,

Abracadabra!

And the garden was ready for the party.
'That was easy,' Winnie said.

'Now what else? Oh yes, I need a surprise.
A good party always has a surprise.
I'll have to think about that.'

Friday the thirteenth was a lovely sunny day,
which was lucky.

At two o'clock Winnie's guests arrived.
'Happy birthday, Winnie,' they shouted,
and they piled up the presents on the lawn.

Wanda, Wilma and Wendy gave
Winnie a magic carpet.
She'd always wanted one of those.

Uncle Owen gave her
a bat in a cage.
She'd never wanted one of those.

Aunty Alice gave her a Book
of Special Spells,

and there was a magic trumpet
from Cousin Cuthbert.

'Let's play some games!' Winnie said.
First they played musical broomsticks.
That was fun, but there was a lot of pushing.
Uncle Owen pushed Aunty Alice into a prickle bush. Ouch!

Cousin Cuthbert bounced off a broomstick and
landed in the fountain. So they let him win.

'Now we'll have a treasure hunt,' said Winnie.

Uncle Owen looked in the maze, and got lost.

Wilma looked in the bat's cage, and the bat flew away.

Wendy looked in the bouncy castle.
Bang!

Wanda found the treasure, but she had some help.

'The next game is hide-and-seek,' Winnie shouted.
But there was so much noise nobody heard her.

So Winnie picked up her new magic trumpet.
Toot, toot, toot,
Winnie tootled . . .

and **everybody** disappeared.
Winnie was surprised.

Then she was cross.
Where had they gone?

Winnie looked
in the maze.
Nobody.

She looked in the
bat's cage.
Nothing.

She looked in the
bouncy castle.
Nobody.

'Blithering broomsticks!' Winnie said.
'Who will eat all my lovely food?'

Then Winnie saw a label on the trumpet.

IMPORTANT:
to make people disappear, toot three times
to make them come back, stand on your head
and toot three times

So Winnie stood on her head.
Toot, toot, toot,
she tootled . . .

and everybody came back, feeling hungry.
They ate up all the food.

'And now it's time for the surprise,' said Winnie.
She opened her new Book of Special Spells.
'Shut your eyes and think about your
favourite cake!' she said.

Everybody shut their eyes.
Aunty Alice thought about chocolate cake.
Uncle Owen thought about fruit cake.
Cousin Cuthbert thought about rainbow cake.
Wilbur thought about cheesecake.
He loved cheesecake.

Then Winnie the Witch shut her eyes,
turned around three times, stamped her foot,
waved her wand, and shouted,

Abracadabra!

And there was the biggest birthday cake
in the whole world,
with candles on the top.

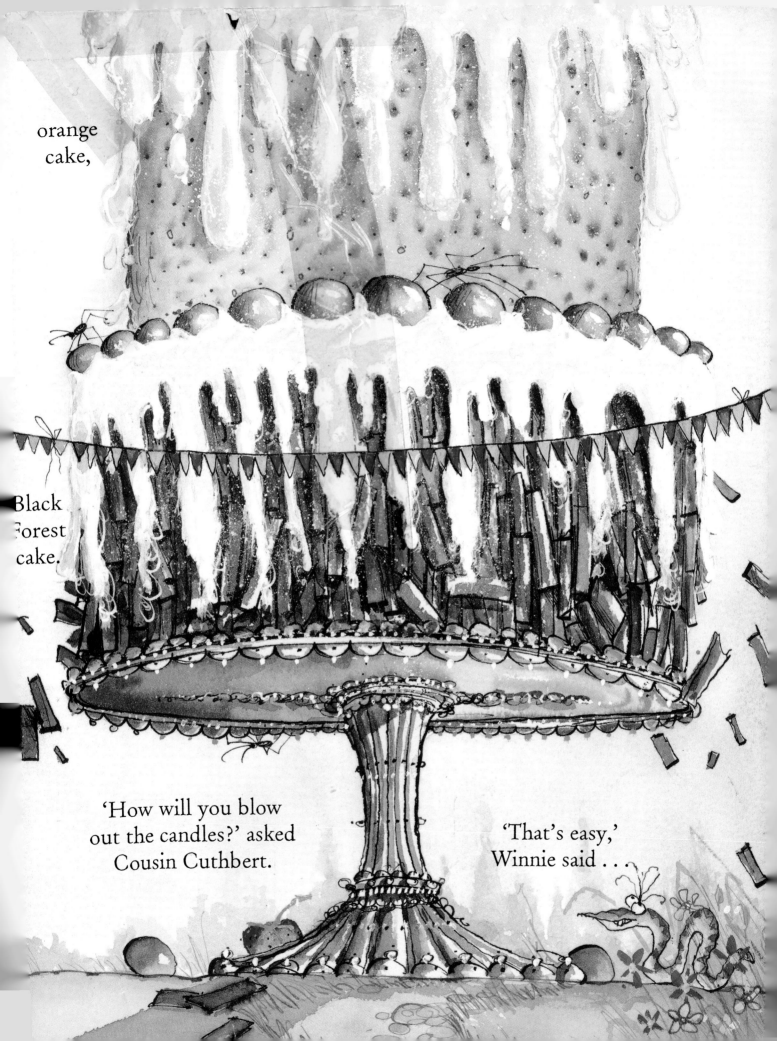

orange cake,

Black Forest cake.

'How will you blow out the candles?' asked Cousin Cuthbert.

'That's easy,' Winnie said . . .

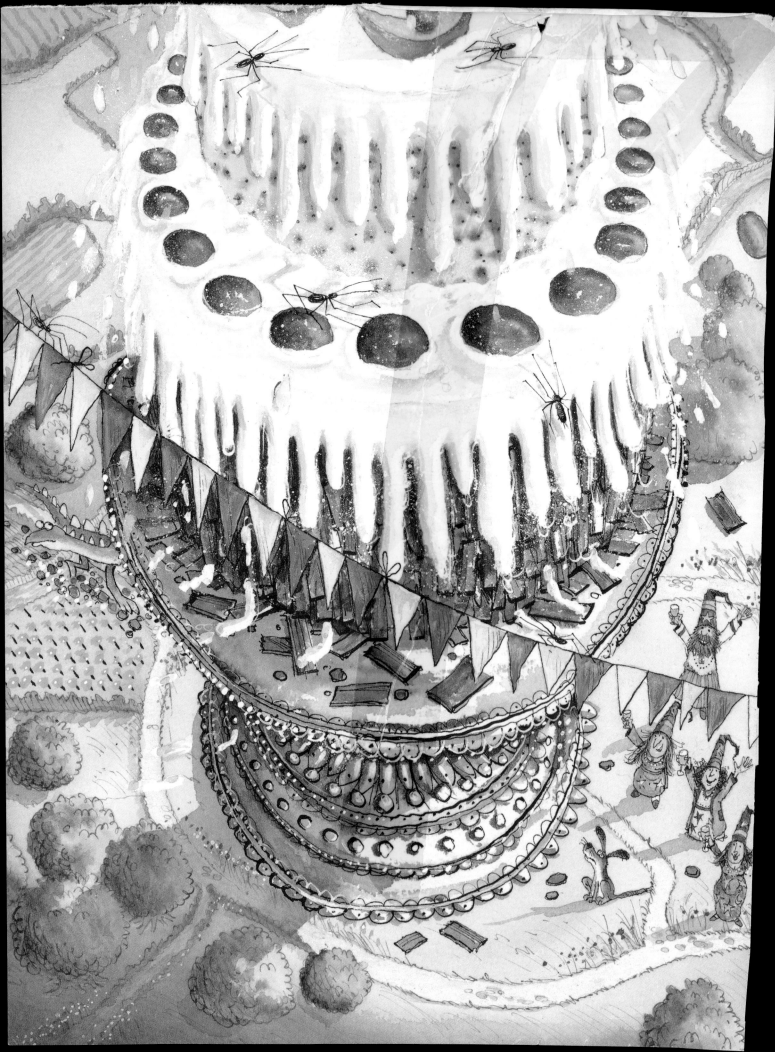

a layer of
cheesecake.

There was
strawberry
shortcake,

ginger
sponge
cake,

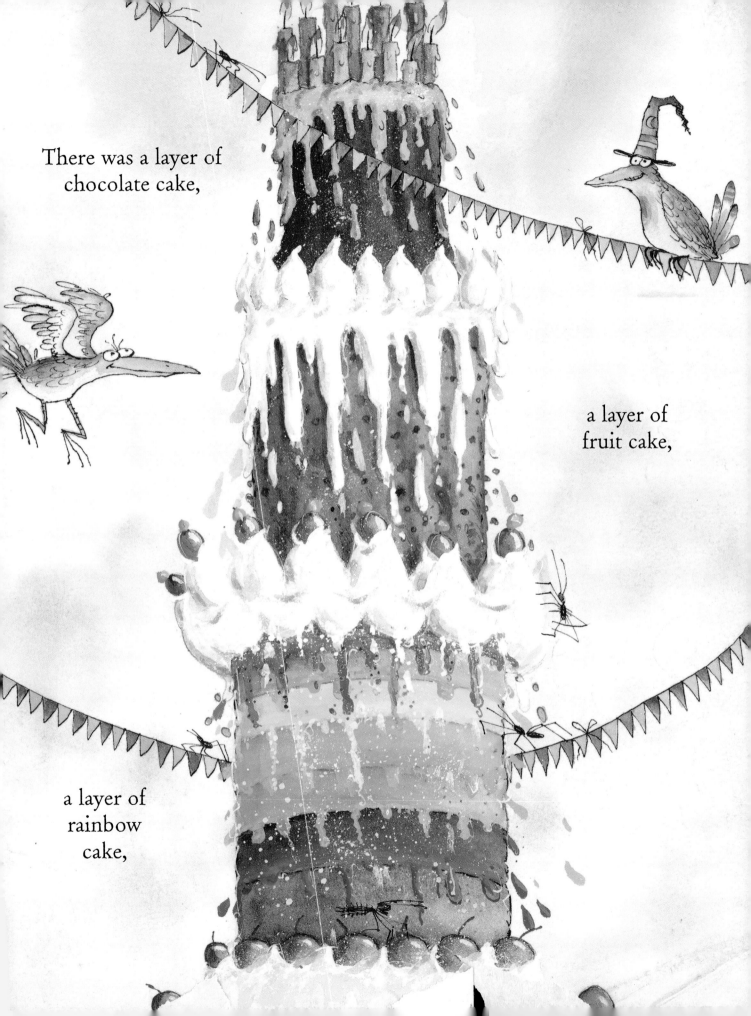

There was a layer of
chocolate cake,

a layer of
fruit cake,

a layer of
rainbow
cake,

and she rode on her magic carpet to the top of the cake.

Puff, puff, puuffffffff!

'Ha ha ha,' laughed Winnie.
'This party is such fun, Wilbur!
I'm a very lucky witch.'

Wilbur didn't say anything.
His mouth was full of cheesecake.
What a lucky black cat!

Happy Birthday to you!